To the generosity
in each of us.

A Gift to Share

The Story of Moritz

Written by

Barry J. Schieber

Illustrated by

Mary Garbe

Silent Moon Books

I was born in a small village high in the snowy Swiss Alps.

I had six brothers and sisters.

Every day we played on the mountainside, chasing each other, rolling down the hill, playing tug-of-war with a towel and chewing on sticks.

Three or four times a day, our mother, Deika, fed us and then we snuggled together and went to sleep.

I loved to look at the snow on the mountains.
I loved to look at the deep blue sky.

One day Mom picked me up
and carried me under the big tree in our yard.

She spoke softly to me.
Soon you will be leaving us
for a new home far away.

You have a gift to share.

You can help to heal people
and make them happy.

This will be your path in life.

Soon visitors will be coming
to meet you.

Find one you know
will be good to you
and who will help you
do your work.
Choose carefully.

She nuzzled me
and licked my nose.

A few days later people began coming to our house,
looking at my brothers and sisters and me.
I didn't pay too much attention.
I was busy running about, eating and napping.

One sunny afternoon a man walked into our yard.
Mom barked.

He looked at her kindly and spoke to her softly.
She stopped barking and wagged her tail.

He seemed gentle and I walked over to him.

He picked me up
and right away
I felt at home in his arms.

He rubbed my belly
and said he would
come see me again.

Days later he returned. He sat on a bench
and watched us playing in the yard.
I scampered over to him and tugged his shoelace.

He laughed.
So we meet again. I think we have a name for you –
Moritz. How does that sound?

To me it was perfect.

Oh yes, he added, *My name is Barry.*

He gave me a big squeeze and whispered in my ear:

Moritz, will you come home with me?

I live far away in Montana. You will have a nice home with a lake, mountains and plenty of room to play.

I put my nose on his nose.

The next morning I said goodbye to my family.
I felt happy to begin my new life.

The airport was noisy and very busy.
At the gate Barry told me I would be okay,
but we would have to be apart until we arrived
in the United States.

Even though my kennel was comfortable,
I was scared.

So I lay down and went to sleep.

When we landed
I was so excited
to see Barry that
I peed on his shoes.

Montana *was* beautiful, with forests, lakes and snow everywhere and such a big blue sky!

We walked along the lake every day.

Barry gave me lots to eat and plenty of treats. And I grew and grew and grew.

One evening we drove to Fort Missoula Park to attend an obedience class with lots of other smaller puppies. They didn't look much like me, but they were a rowdy bunch and lots of fun, jumping all over the place and running in all directions. No wonder we needed an obedience class!

Somehow when I was around they all seemed to calm down a bit.

I loved my new home. Everywhere we went
people were so friendly. They came over to say hello,
to pet or play with me. I made lots of new friends.

On my first birthday Barry said,
*How would you like to go to the hospital
and visit patients? I think you would be
good at this work.*

The way Barry spoke to me,
I felt it would be another
interesting adventure.

We drove to the hospital in Missoula
where they put me through some tests
to see if I could become a Pet Therapy Dog.

The tests would show if I could cope
with many different situations.

I saw chairs with wheels.
I saw machines that beeped.
People argued and shouted at
each other. Some walked with crutches.
Some waved their arms and
then hugged me too hard.
Some wore funny hats or
bandages on their heads.

I was not one bit scared.
I wagged my tail.

Therapy Dog
Test Today

It was fun – even here people seemed
to slow down and become more quiet
when they were with me.

I remembered my mother's words:
Giving is your path in life.

Could this be it? It seemed so simple.
I wondered if anything so easy
could really be my life's work.

Early one morning we jumped in the car.

I love sunrise when the sky is pink and blue.
I put my nose out the window
and I smell the morning air – pine trees,
flowers, deer, even bears!

When I saw the hospital I knew I had passed
the test. I was a real Pet Therapy Dog!
Before we went in, Barry said to me:
*Moritz, you have a gift. Please share it
with everyone we meet.*

As we walked down the hallway
to visit our first patient, everyone stopped
to talk to me, laughing and giving me hugs.

We were invited into our first room.

I saw a small child in a big bed.

He looked lost. He had a sky blue cast
on both legs from his toes to his hips,
plastic tubes attached to the back of his hand,
wires from his chest to a big monitor.
He had a white bandage around his head.
Above the bandage his blond hair stuck
straight up.

The little boy looked frightened.
I walked over to greet him.

I put my nose on his hand, then on his chest.
Finally I put my nose right on his nose.

The little boy began to cry.
I pulled back a little and looked at him,
thinking, *Don't be afraid. We are friends.*

He looked at me
and stopped crying.

He looked again
and his big blue eyes
began to sparkle
and he laughed.

I lay down by his bed.

After awhile Barry and I left
to visit other patients, some old
and some young.

They all seemed to like us.
So every Tuesday, for over a year,
we continued these visits.

Each day after we left the hospital
Barry and I would walk in the park.

I would look up to the deep blue sky
and remember my mother's words:
You have a gift to share.

I think we all have a gift to share.

What do you think yours is?

Silent Moon Books

Post Office Box 1865, Bigfork, Montana 59911

For additional information on Moritz's adventures,

pet therapy, and news for the heart visit:

www.nose-to-nose.com

ORDERS AND INFORMATION CONTACT:

info@ nose-to-nose.com.

A portion of the proceeds from the sale of *A Gift to Share*

will be donated to animal welfare projects.

ISBN 0-9721457-1-0

Printed in China